To P&J + A
Thank you for always
encouraging me.
L, KA

**Ruby the Rainbow Witch:
A Picture-Perfect Rainbow Day**

Published by: Lucky Four Press, 2019
Copyright © 2019 Kim Ann / Lucky Four Press
Library of Congress Control Number: 2019910144

Printed in the USA.

All inquires should be directed to
luckyfourpress@yahoo.com

ISBN-13: 978-1-7339380-0-6 paperback
ISBN-13: 978-1-7339380-1-3 hardcover

LUCKY FOUR
PRESS

Ruby the Rainbow Witch

Written by Kim Ann

Illustrated by Nejla Shojaie

This is Ruby the Rainbow Witch.

She wears a rainbow dress and a picture-perfect rainbow hat.

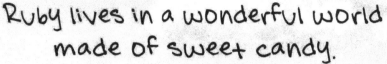

Ruby lives in a wonderful world
made of sweet candy.

There is a lazy lemonade river and puffy
purple and big blue cotton candy clouds.

It is the most picture-perfect
place you could ever see!

One magical day, Ruby went for a wonderful whirly walk down Pastry Path.

She came across a friendly frog. He was sitting in a comfy chair made of gooey gumdrops.

He looked at Ruby and said, "Hello, my name is Fudge the Frog. I like your hat!"

"Oh, thank you! My name is Ruby the Rainbow Witch, and this is my picture perfect rainbow hat."

"I love it," said Fudge. "I wish I had a picture-perfect rainbow hat too!"

"As you wishy-wish," she said. With a whirl and twirl of her rainbow dress and a wave of her swirly-whirly wand, POOF, Fudge now had his very own picture-perfect rainbow hat.

"Thank you Ruby. You have made this the most picture-perfect rainbow day!"

Ruby smiled and went on her
wonderful whirly way.

Ruby came across a cuddly cat laying by Peppermint Palace.

She looked at Ruby and said, "Hello, my name is Cocoa the Cat. I like your hat!".

"Oh, thank you! My name is Ruby the Rainbow Witch, and this is my picture-perfect rainbow hat."

"I love it," said Cocoa. "I wish I had a picture-perfect rainbow hat too!"

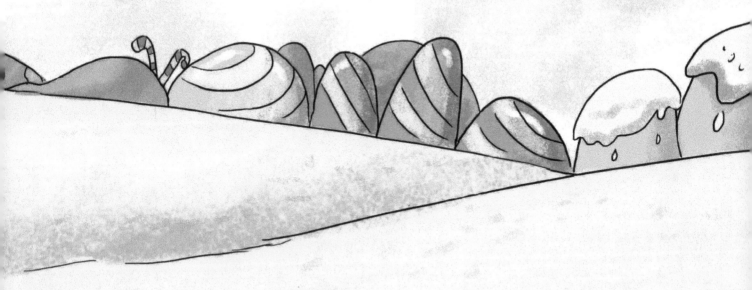

"As you wishy-wish," she said. With a whirl and twirl of her rainbow dress and a wave of her swirly-whirly wand, POOF, Cocoa now had her very own picture-perfect rainbow hat.

"Thank you Ruby. You have made this the most picture-perfect rainbow day!"

Ruby smiled and went on her
wonderful whirly way.

Ruby came across a bouncy bunny
playing in Marshmallow Meadow.

He looked at Ruby and said, "Hello,
my name is Butterscotch the Bunny.
I like your hat!"

"Oh, thank you! My name is Ruby the Rainbow Witch, and this is my picture-perfect rainbow hat."

"I love it," said Butterscotch. "I wish I had a picture-perfect rainbow hat too!"

"As you wishy-wish," she said. With a whirl and twirl of her rainbow dress and a wave of her swirly-whirly wand, POOF, Butterscotch now had his very own picture-perfect rainbow hat.

"Thank you Ruby. You have made this the most picture-perfect rainbow day!"

Ruby thought about how fabulously fun it was making new friends and helping others.

"Friendly friends are my favorite way to make a picture-perfect rainbow day!" said Ruby.

She smiled and went on her
wonderful whirly way.

About the Author

Kim Ann was born in Massachusetts and now lives
in Southern California with her husband,
her two teenagers, and their dogs.

For several years, Kim Ann worked as a freelance writer
and published many feel-good articles about families,
but she dreamed of writing the fun, imaginative,
colorful books she liked reading to her own children.

Kim Ann is the author of the
"Ruby the Rainbow Witch" book series:

"Ruby the Rainbow Witch: A Picture-Perfect Rainbow Day"
"Ruby the Rainbow Witch: The Lost Swirly-Whirly Wand"

and looks forward to writing more Ruby adventures!

_____